GODDESS STAR

Balboa Press books may be ordered through booksellers or by contacting:

Balboa Press
A Division of Hay House
1663 Liberty Drive
Bloomington, IN 47403
www.balboapress.com
1 (877) 407-4847

Because of the dynamic nature of the Internet, any web addresses or links contained in this book may have changed since publication and may no longer be valid. The views expressed in this work are solely those of the author and do not necessarily reflect the views of the publisher, and the publisher hereby disclaims any responsibility for them.

Any people depicted in stock imagery provided by Getty Images are models, and such images are being used for illustrative purposes only. Certain stock imagery © Getty Images.

ISBN: 978-1-9822-1084-7 (sc)
ISBN: 978-1-9822-1083-0 (e)

Library of Congress Control Number: 2018910151

Print information available on the last page.

Balboa Press rev. date: 09/20/2018

BALBOA
PRESS
A DIVISION OF HAY HOUSE

GODDESS STAR

S. C. INAHARA

For Nico, who inspires me everyday.

For my AAAC, a Goddess Star
beyond measure, who has always
shown me the Light.

To all those who have survived being bullied.
May our light shine on!

"There are several kinds of love. One is a selfish, mean, grasping, egotistical thing which uses love for self-importance. This is the ugly and crippling kind. The other is an outpouring of everything good in you — of kindness and consideration and respect — not only the social respect of manners but the greater respect which is recognition of another person as unique and valuable. The first kind can make you sick and small and weak but the second can release in you strength, and courage and goodness and even wisdom you didn't know you had."

-John Steinbeck: A Life In Letters

"And until you stand as the light that you are, you will not feel complete."

- Dr. Christiane Northrup,
Dodging Energy Vampires

Once upon a time, there was a bully named Rumpus.

Rumpus was top dog of important affairs. At first glance, he was like a mosquito, tiny and seemingly inconsequential.

But he knew just how to hide in order to conceal his true nature.

Rumpus was a clever and devious manipulator. He sometimes got thirsty for mean stuff, and when he did, he puffed up and displayed a most despicable version of himself.

What he didn't know was that soon, there would be a Goddess Star in his lowly life.

Goddess Star was a very special being. She shined brightly, because her heart was filled with Love and Goodness from the Universe, and she glowed like a galaxy of stars.

One day, while performing her duties, Goddess Star met Rumpus. Every day, she would attempt to walk beside him as his equal, and did her best to assuage his bullying disposition.

Goddess Star held integrity to its highest measure. When she saw that Rumpus had neither heart nor soul, and relished in beastly deeds, her light began to fade.

Time passed and Rumpus' terrible malice began to burble and rumble in his belly, like a chef's pot of boiling pig's feet! It had laid dormant in a feverish and irritable slumber, impatiently resurfacing with an evil that was apparent to few. He could contain it no longer.

What Goddess Star did not understand was that Rumpus was in love with his own heartless, unkind self, a self devoid of feeling, empathy, and authenticity. Some had tried to unmask him, but without success. Perhaps there was no true Rumpus, after all...only emptiness.

One day Goddess Star went about her business, but from her good and unsuspecting heart, did not see the evil that was about to happen.

The night before, Rumpus cried so deeply in his soul, that he did not even hear his own sadness, nor see his own tears, flowing uncontrollably down to his toes, puddling around his feet.

He was filled with jealous scorn because in his deep down soul, he could see Goddess Star's peace and light.

He wanted to steal that light for himself, and so Rumpus summoned his vile and contemptible ways.

He devised a callous, cruel scheme and began to break Goddess Star. She faltered and weakened. Rumpus smiled a sinister smile and rubbed his hands together, the gift of human compassion meaningless to him.

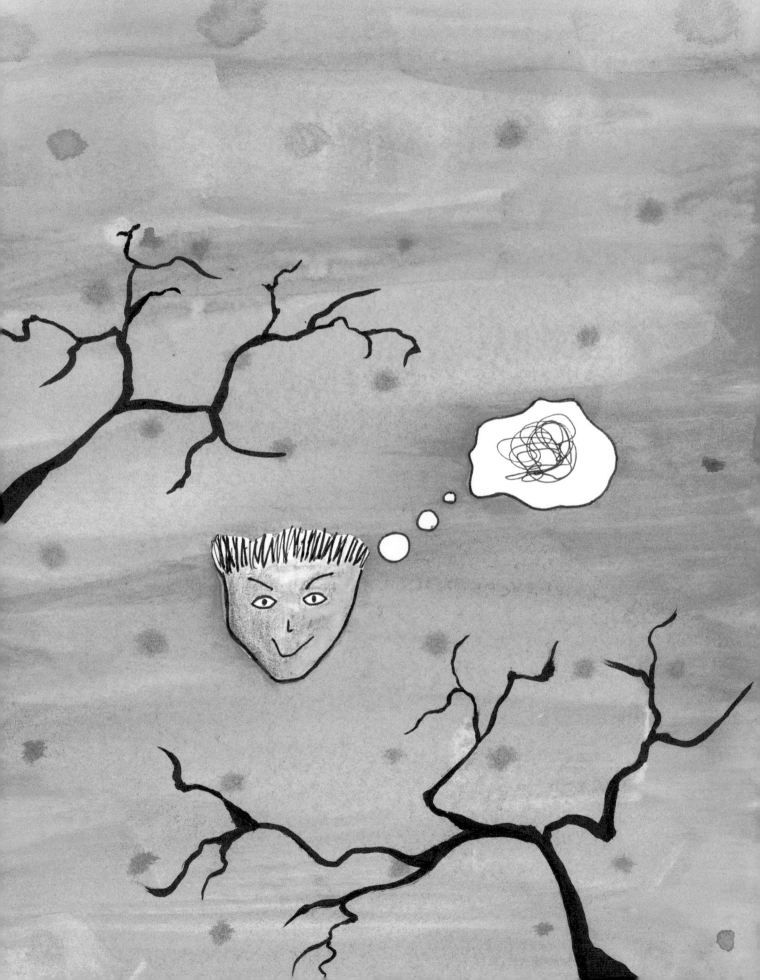

Goddess Star departed, broken, and sought comfort in sleep. She slept for 20 days and 20 nights, and during that steadfast slumber, she had a dream.

She dreamed that she was holding hands with all the people who had touched her life. In her dream were the hearts and souls of all those who had embraced her, laughed with her, loved her.

She dreamed of Strength and Goodness and Light, and from this sprouted new, fresh seeds of positivity, revelation, and vision.

When Goddess Star awoke from her deep sleep, she felt warm inside and radiated golden light.

She understood the importance of honoring and nurturing herself in order to regain her power. Goddess Star then drew a line to forever bar Rumpus from her heart. She was thankful that someone so wicked could show her a new path to her own self!

Rumpus was bewildered and overcome by her brilliant light that spoke so much truth. He fell, cast down in the shadows of his own darkness.

The more she glowed, the more he retreated in shadow, until he was a mere sliver of himself. The dark sliver glared at her, and scampered away, exposed and shamed. And then, he disappeared into obscurity.

Goddess Star became the One she was meant to be...her True Self! She danced a little dance in a dazzling blue flower dress, down the path, over the hill, and around the bend to begin her new journey.

About the Author

S.C. Inahara is from the Pacific Northwest. In addition to a career working with children, she is also a former chef. She enjoys the arts in all their forms, and has great reverance for the creative mind, and the goodness and light of Goddess Stars everywhere!

Printed in the United States
By Bookmasters